by Monica Hare

illustrated by Ian Johnson

I had a dream that yesterday was
a warm sunny day. The brightly
coloured songbirds meowed sweetly
in the cotton wool trees as I drove
down a country lane in my bright
pink knitted car.

You could just see the paper moon fading in the sky next to a large beaming sunflower.

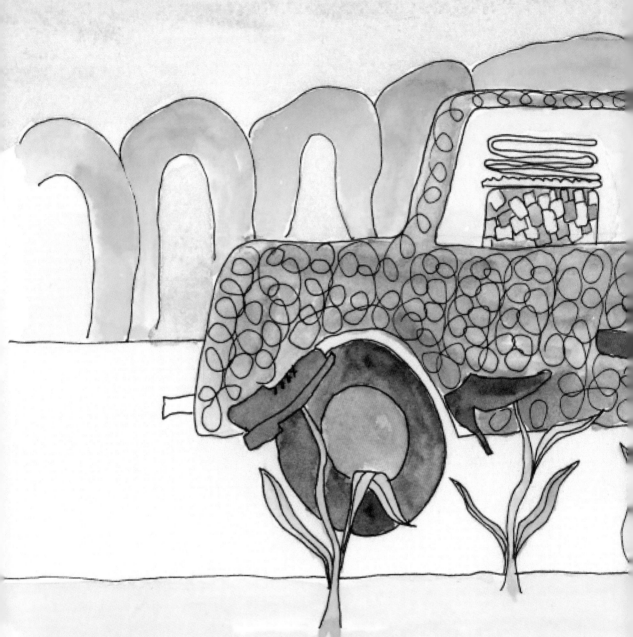

Jumpers, my marmalade cross-eyed cross-stitched cat, sat contentedly on the seat beside me with a large grin on his face. A brightly coloured patchwork picnic basket and mohair rug were on the back seat.

We gently passed the looped hedgerows and flowers made different shoes. Jumpers w

When it was time for lunch we
opped by a large treacle lily. I
ok out crocheted cups, plates and
lery from the basket.

We ate our favourite seaweed sandwiches and drank saltwater lemonade.

After lunch was Jumper's favourite part of the day, because he went for a swim in the treacle pond...

...followed by a sunbathe on a lily and a good lick of his paws; at which point his grin became even broader.

I took my knitting out and made a few houses with smoking chimneys.

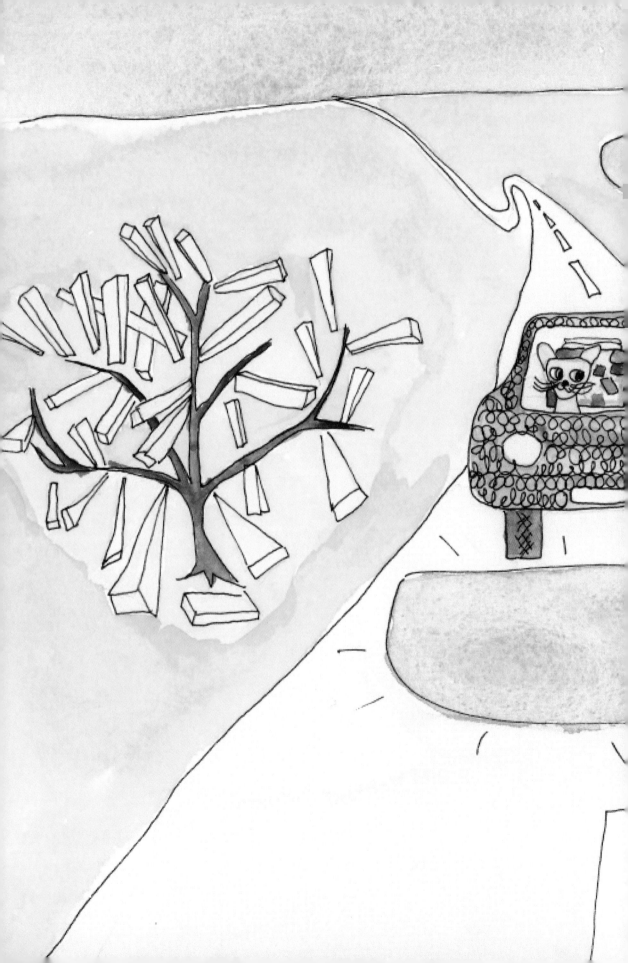

We got back into the car and drove past fields of fish and chips. Suddenly there was an enormous puddle.

We got out, I unravelled the car...

...picked up the picnic basket and rug, then leapt over the puddle.

It didn't take long to re-knit the car...

...and go merrily home for tea.

The end

14179921R00015

Printed in Great Britain
by Amazon